Welcome to ALADDIN QUIX!

If you are looking for fast, fun-to-read stories with colorful characters, lots of kid-friendly humor, easy-to-follow action, entertaining story lines, and lively illustrations, then **ALADDIN QUIX** is for you!

But wait, there's more!

If you're also looking for stories with tables of contents; word lists; about-the-book questions; 64, 80, or 96 pages; short chapters; short paragraphs; and large fonts, then **ALADDIN QUIX** is *definitely* for you!

ALADDIN QUIX: The next step between ready to reads and longer, more challenging chapter books, for readers five to eight years old.

Read all the books in the Royal Sweets series!

ROYAL SWEETS

Rainbow Surprise

By Helen Perelman

Illustrated by Olivia Chin Mueller

ALADDIN QUIX

New York   London   Toronto   Sydney   New Delhi

For Nora and Lucy Connelly —H. P.

ALADDIN QUIX
Simon & Schuster Children's Publishing Division
1230 Avenue of the Americas, New York, New York 10020
First Aladdin QUIX hardcover edition September 2022
Text copyright © 2022 by Helen Perelman
Illustrations copyright © 2022 by Olivia Chin Mueller
Also available in an Aladdin QUIX paperback edition.
All rights reserved, including the right of reproduction in whole or in part in any form.
ALADDIN and the related marks and colophon are trademarks of Simon & Schuster, Inc.
For information about special discounts for bulk purchases, please contact
Simon & Schuster Special Sales at 1-866-506-1949 or business@simonandschuster.com.
The Simon & Schuster Speakers Bureau can bring authors to your live event. For more
information or to book an event contact the Simon & Schuster Speakers Bureau
at 1-866-248-3049 or visit our website at www.simonspeakers.com.
Series designed by Jessica Handelman
Book designed by Tiara Iandiorio
The illustrations for this book were rendered digitally.
The text of this book was set in Archer Medium.
Manufactured in the United States of America 0822 LAK
2 4 6 8 10 9 7 5 3 1
Library of Congress Control Number 2022936554
ISBN 9781534476240 (hc)
ISBN 9781534476233 (pbk)
ISBN 9781534476257 (ebook)

Cast of Characters

Princess Mini: Royal fairy princess of Candy Kingdom

Gobo: Troll living in Sugar Valley

Butterscotch: Princess Mini's royal unicorn

Princess Cupcake and Prince Frosting: Princess Mini's twin cousins from Cake Kingdom

Princess Sprinkle: Princess Mini's aunt and ruler of Cake Kingdom

Princess Flour: Princess Mini's older cousin

Jelly: Princess Flour's royal unicorn

Sparkle: Baby unicorn

Queen Sweetie and King Crunch: Princess Mini's grandparents

Princess Taffy: Princess Mini's best friend

Sugarpop: Prince Frosting's royal unicorn

Chipper: Princess Taffy's royal unicorn

Princess Lolli and Prince Scoop: Princess Mini's parents and ruling fairies of Candy Kingdom

Contents

1

Rainbow Star

I, **Princess Mini**, was super excited. My good friend **Gobo** and I were on our way to Cake Kingdom. We were going to see a baby unicorn!

"Almost there!" I called to

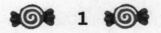

Gobo. Gobo was a troll who lived in Chocolate Woods. He sat behind me on **Butterscotch**'s back.

"Look, I can see my house!" Gobo exclaimed. He pointed below as we passed over Chocolate Woods.

Butterscotch followed Chocolate River up past Caramel Hills and over Chocolate Falls.

Cake Kingdom was north of Candy Kingdom, where we lived. My cousins **Princess Cupcake** and **Prince Frosting** lived there in a castle with my aunt, **Princess**

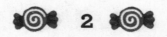

Sprinkle, and their older sister, **Princess Flour**. Cupcake and Frosting were in my classroom at Royal Fairy Academy. Sometimes Cupcake wasn't so sweet, and Frosting liked to play tricks,

but we were all friends.

"I see the castle!" Gobo exclaimed, pointing.

The large, round chocolate castle was up ahead. Cake Castle was in the shape of a cupcake.

"It's choc-o-rific!" I exclaimed.

"I have never been to another kingdom in Sugar Valley," Gobo said.

"You are going to *love* Cake Kingdom," I told him.

Visiting my cousins and my aunt in Cake Kingdom was always fun. Princess Sprinkle was my mother's sister. She ruled over the Candy Fairies in Cake Kingdom. Her castle was next to Cupcake Lake, surrounded by cupcake gardens filled with many candy flowers and trees. Cake Kingdom was a delicious place to visit!

"I can't wait to meet the new unicorn," I said.

"Me too!" Gobo shouted.

Princess Flour's unicorn, **Jelly**, had a baby, and Cupcake and Frosting were taking care of her.

Butterscotch landed in the **paddock** near the stables. Frosting and Cupcake flew over to us.

"Come quick!" Frosting shouted.

6

"She might be sleeping," Cupcake said, turning to us. She put her finger to her lips. "So be quiet."

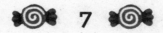

Sometimes Cupcake could be bossy, but I knew it was important to be quiet if the baby was sleeping.

In the first stall, I saw Jelly. She was a large blue unicorn with a pink **mane** and tail. Her horn and hooves were sparkly gold. Jelly was keeping careful watch over her baby.

"There she is," whispered Cupcake.

I looked closer. In a **heap** of hay, I saw a tiny unicorn with laven-

der wings and a vanilla coat. Her mane and tail were made up of silky rainbow strands.

"Look at her tiny hooves," I said, pointing. "They are the prettiest lavender."

"She is so small," Gobo added.

"What is her name?" I asked.

"**Sparkle**," Cupcake said, smiling. "Flour said I could name her."

"That is a **rainbow-licious** name!" I exclaimed. I moved closer to the baby unicorn. "Hello, Sparkle!"

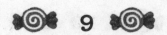

"She is not just *your* unicorn, Cupcake," Frosting spat.

"I know," Cupcake said. Then she **smirked**. "She is kinda."

"No," Frosting said firmly.

Sparkle lifted her head.

"I think she likes her name," I told them. "And she probably doesn't like you fighting."

Sparkle tried to stand on her skinny legs. She **wobbled** and then fell.

"Has she been flying yet?" I asked.

Frosting shook his head. "No."

"You have to walk before you fly," I said to the tiny unicorn.

Gobo petted Sparkle's long neck. "She smells like vanilla," he said, smiling.

"Is Sparkle going to the Rainbow Jubilee?" I asked.

Our grandparents, **Queen Sweetie** and **King Crunch**, were hosting a Rainbow Jubilee for their wedding anniversary. Candy Fairies from all the kingdoms were going to Sugar Kingdom for the party. I knew Flour was riding Jelly in the unicorn show. I wondered if Frosting and Cupcake wanted to **showcase** Sparkle.

"If we can train her to fly," Cupcake said. "Flour is busy with getting Jelly ready for the show."

"Training is hard work," Frosting said.

Cupcake took a brush to Sparkle's mane. "She would make the best rainbow surprise at the jubilee," she told them.

 12

"The jubilee is in two weeks," Gobo said.

"Exactly," Frosting said, rolling his eyes. "That is not a ton of time to train her."

"Remember Lady Cherry told us about the famous unicorn wizard Blue Bell?" I said.

"Yes!" Cupcake cried. "Blue Bell trained a herd of unicorns."

"She was a wizard," Frosting added. "She had special magic."

"We can do it," I said. "What do you think, Sparkle?"

Sparkle **nuzzled** my hand.

I took that as a good sign.

"We will make you the star of the Rainbow Jubilee!" I said.

2

Chocolate Bark

Gobo and I flew over to Cake Kingdom after school the next day. I asked **Princess Taffy** to come too. She was my best friend and always eager to help. With only two weeks to train Sparkle,

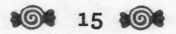

we needed all the help we could get!

When we arrived, Sparkle was **grazing** on sugar vines growing in the paddock.

"She is **sugar-tastic**!" Taffy said. "Her mane and tail are so pretty! She is every color of the rainbow!"

Cupcake and Frosting flew over to us.

"Thanks for coming," Frosting said. "Sparkle is still not flying."

"I think she looks bigger than

yesterday," I said. "Maybe today she will try to fly."

"I hope so," Cupcake said. "Flour doesn't think she will be ready for the jubilee."

Gobo took a chocolate treat out of his pocket. "I know unicorns like chocolate bark," he said. "Maybe she will like this?" He held out his hand for Sparkle to smell the treat.

Sparkle's tail swished left and right. Her brown eyes opened wider. She nibbled on the chocolate bark.

"She likes it!" Frosting exclaimed.

"I have more," Gobo said. He patted his pocket. "I am not a wizard, but I know unicorns like chocolate."

"Me too," Frosting said. He held out his hand.

Gobo laughed. "These treats are for Sparkle."

"I move faster when there is a treat," Frosting said. He flapped his wings and made a loop in the sky, like a unicorn.

Sparkle's brown eyes followed Frosting as he leaped up in the air.

"Come on, Sparkle," Taffy said. "Flap your wings for more chocolate."

As much as Sparkle liked the chocolate, her wings did not move. She lowered her head to the ground.

Gobo walked over to me. "How did you learn to fly?" he asked.

I thought about that for a moment. "I don't know," I said. "My wings started moving, and then I flew."

We looked over at Sparkle. Her rainbow wings were **drooping** on the ground.

Taffy reached into her bag and held up a book. "I took out this book from the school library today," she said. She showed us the book: *Training Your Unicorn.*

She opened the book. "Chapter one is about getting your unicorn to feel **comfortable**."

"She looks pretty comfortable," Frosting said. Sparkle was lying in the grass in the middle of a flower patch. "She's eating all the sugar flowers."

"Maybe something is wrong with her wings?" Cupcake asked. "She isn't moving them at all."

"I don't think anything is wrong," Frosting said. He shrugged. "She doesn't want to fly."

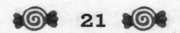

Cupcake crossed her arms over her chest. "What makes you so sure?"

Frosting put his hands on his hips. "You don't know anything," he said.

I didn't want to hear Frosting and Cupcake argue. Sometimes they are like a sour lemon-lime candy. I had to think of something.

I suggested, "Seeing how other unicorns fly might help her."

"There is a chapter about that, too!" Taffy said. She held up the

book. There was a picture of two unicorns with a baby unicorn flying next to them.

Cupcake sighed, and Frosting **grunted**.

"Let's try," I said.

Butterscotch was resting in Cupcake Meadow with Jelly. I called to them, and they flew over to us. Jelly came over to Sparkle and gently nudged her.

Sparkle didn't move. She was still more interested in the sugar flowers. Butterscotch and Jelly flew around the paddock and then settled back down in the meadow to rest.

I wasn't sure if Sparkle was sleepy or scared. But I did know

that training her to fly for the
unicorn show at the jubilee
was going to be harder than we
thought.

3

A Great Idea

After two weeks of after-school visits to Cake Kingdom, Sparkle was still not flying, and Frosting and Cupcake were fighting more.

"What are we going to do?"

Taffy asked. We were sitting in the paddock, watching Sparkle nibble on sugar flowers. "The jubilee is tomorrow."

"I know," I said. **"This is super sour."**

"Maybe we should send for a wizard," Gobo said.

Cupcake and Frosting didn't want to call a wizard, though. They wanted to do the training on their own.

No one thought Sparkle was sick. She just didn't want to fly.

The twins flew into the paddock with snacks for us. Their sad faces made me want to help even more.

"Blue Bell used to sing to her unicorns," I said. "We haven't tried that yet."

"Singing would keep the unicorns relaxed," Taffy said.

Gobo started to sing a song, and we joined in. *"Sugar flowers on the hill,"* he sang. Sparkle's tiny ears straightened as she listened to the song. She walked over, moving closer to us.

I held my breath.

I hoped her wings would start to flap.

 29

When the song ended, Sparkle closed her eyes and settled back down in the grass.

"If she were more relaxed, she would be sleeping," Frosting said. He kneeled down next to Sparkle. "She is asleep!"

"Babies do sleep most of the time," Taffy told him.

"I think Sparkle is scared," Cupcake said. "If we only knew what she was scared about, maybe we could help."

Gobo agreed. "I would be

scared of flying," he said.

"That's because you don't have wings," Frosting said.

"I guess," Gobo said sadly. "If I did have wings, I would fly!"

Cupcake snapped her fingers. "Wait!" she said. She flew to the barn and took a long red licorice rope from a hook. "Maybe we can help her move her wings."

We put a **harness** on Sparkle and attached the long licorice rope around her wings.

"Pull the rope so she can feel

her wings move," Cupcake said. "Come on, Sparkle!"

When Sparkle swished her tail and not her wings, Cupcake dropped the rope. "Poor baby," she said. She petted Sparkle's neck and gave her a tight hug. "I wish I knew how to help you."

"She is not going to fly," said Frosting. He sat down and put his head in his hands. "And she is not going to be in the show."

"I have another idea," Gobo said, jumping up. "Sparkle can be

in a float for the unicorn show. She could just stand." Gobo looked over at Sparkle. "Or lie down."

"Gobo!" I cried. "That is a **choc-o-rific** idea!"

"Yes!" Cupcake cheered. "She wouldn't have to fly and could still be in the show."

Frosting slowly shook his head. "Everyone would wonder why she wasn't flying," he said.

"Maybe," I said. "But at least she would be at the celebration. Grandma Sweetie and Grandpa Crunch would love to see a baby unicorn. Everyone would love that."

I knew this wasn't the best

solution, but at least we could bring Sparkle to the jubilee. I smiled at Gobo. He was a good friend with a great idea!

We started working on a float for Sparkle.

We used cupcake wrappers and covered branches of a gummy tree.

Then we tied red licorice ropes to finish off the float.

Butterscotch and **Sugarpop** would pull the carriage for Sparkle's ride around Sugar Kingdom.

Cupcake had the idea to make a banner. We painted "Happy Rainbow Jubilee!" on a long red fruit leather strip with white frosting and sprinkles.

"This is sugar-tastic!" Taffy exclaimed.

HAPPY RAINBOW JUBILEE!

"I know Grandma Sweetie and Grandpa Crunch will love this," I said.

"Yes," Cupcake said. She still looked sad. This wasn't how she wanted Sparkle to go to the jubilee.

"Sparkle might surprise us," I told her.

I crossed my fingers behind my back and made a wish for Sparkle to fly.

4

Sugar Kingdom

The next day, I went to Sugar Kingdom with my cousins. We were going to have a royal sleepover at the castle before the jubilee. We flew on our unicorns and followed Flour and

Jelly, who pulled a carriage for Sparkle.

Sugar Castle was the largest castle in Sugar Valley. There were four tall **turrets** that surrounded a wide courtyard. Each turret had colorful sugar stones on the very

top. A large **drawbridge** was at the entrance of the castle, to allow visitors to cross over the chocolate **moat**.

I saw my grandpa in the courtyard. He was waving at us.

"Welcome to Sugar Kingdom!" Grandpa Crunch called. "I am so happy to see my grandfairies!"

"Hello!" we sang out.

"We are so happy to be here," I told him. I stretched my arms out wide. "Happy Rainbow Jubilee!"

"Thank you," he said.

He leaned over to see inside the carriage. Maybe he thought there was something in there for him? I had to think fast. We didn't want him to see Sparkle before the jubilee.

"Do you want to hear a song we learned at school?" I asked.

Cupcake knew what I was doing. "Come over here, Grandpa," she said. She took his hand and flew over to a bench, away from the carriage.

We sang a song Lord Licorice had taught us about the Rainbow Jubilee. Grandpa tapped his foot on the ground as we sang. Frosting was singing softly, but Cupcake and I knew all the words and tried to sing loudly.

"Bravo!" Grandpa Crunch cheered. He clapped his hands. "I am so happy you are here early. This is going to be a very special celebration."

"Sure as sugar!" I agreed.

"We should take our unicorns to the stables," Frosting said.

"Yes, go ahead," Grandpa Crunch told us. "Get settled, and I will tell your grandma that you are here."

"I bet she is busy with all the decorations," Cupcake said.

"Yes," Grandpa said. "Lots

of rainbow decorations for the Rainbow Jubilee!" He turned and flew off into the castle. "See you at dinner!"

"Sparkle will fit right in," I said. "Look at all those rainbow flags!"

"If only she would fly around the courtyard like all the other unicorns," Cupcake said.

Cupcake's and Frosting's wings were dragging, and I felt terrible. I had to do something. When we got to the stables, I gave Sparkle a sugar carrot. "Do you want to practice?" I asked.

"She looks more like she wants to take a nap," Cupcake said.

I petted Sparkle's head. Her coat was so soft.

Frosting grabbed the carrot from me and took a bite. "I don't think she wants to do much of anything," he said.

"This was a sour idea," Cupcake said. She crossed her arms across her chest. "No other unicorn is on a float. They are all flying in the show and doing fantastic tricks."

I realized that we had to stop trying to get Sparkle to do something. She had to want to fly.

"I think we should leave her alone," I said. "Let's go out to the castle and check back on her later. She will be fine here with the other unicorns."

Sparkle looked at us with her large brown eyes.

"You'll figure it out," I whispered to her.

I flew after my cousins to have dinner at the castle.

5

Spectacular!

Gobo and Taffy met us in Sugar Kingdom the next morning. Sugar Valley was buzzing with excitement. Today was the Rainbow Jubilee! Candy Fairies and unicorns from all over Sugar

Valley were at Candy Castle gathering for the jubilee.

I was so happy to see Taffy and Gobo. **Chipper** had flown them to Sugar Kingdom, and they met me at the stables.

"I think Cupcake is going to have a meltdown if Sparkle doesn't fly," Taffy said.

Gobo walked over to Sparkle. "I brought you more chocolate bark," he said. "This bark has some sprinkles."

Sparkle took the chocolate, but

her wings were flat against her
back.

"Look!" Taffy exclaimed.

Sparkle's wings started to flut-
ter. They moved slowly at first and
then faster.

"I think she is trying to fly!" Gobo said.

"Were those magic sprinkles?" I asked.

Gobo shook his head. "No, just rainbow," he said. "I thought Sparkle would like them."

I moved closer to Sparkle. "You can do it," I said, cheering her on. "I will fly right next to you."

"What is happening?" Frosting asked. He and Cupcake flew into the stable.

"Sparkle is flapping her wings!"

Cupcake cried. "She's off the ground!"

As Sparkle moved her wings, her horn changed from lavender to a blend of rainbow colors.

Her horn was a rainbow spectacular!

"Sweet sugars!" I cried. "Look at her horn!"

I couldn't believe what I was seeing. Sparkle's horn got brighter and brighter as her wings moved.

"What is happening?" Frosting asked, scratching his head.

"Sparkle is a rainbow unicorn!" Cupcake said, clapping her hands.

"What is a rainbow unicorn?" Frosting asked. His mouth dropped open. "Is she sick?"

"Don't you ever listen to Lady Cherry?" Cupcake scolded. She shot him a frosty look.

Frosting shrugged. "Sometimes," he said.

"No, Sparkle isn't sick," she told him. "She is **unique**!"

"A unicorn with a rainbow horn is very special," I said. "I can't believe it!"

"A rainbow unicorn is good luck," Taffy added.

"Grandma Sweetie is going

to love her," I said. "This is **rainbow-licious**!"

"I knew you would fly when you wanted," I whispered to Sparkle when she landed. Her tail swished from side to side.

Frosting petted Sparkle's neck. "Come on, Sparkle," he said gently. "Fly next to me." He fluttered his wings and flew in front of her.

And just like that, Sparkle moved her wings up and down and lifted off the ground again,

her beautiful rainbow horn glow-
ing bright.

Sparkle was flying!

And she was on her way to
being the star of the show!

 55

6

Rainbow-licious

My cousins and I changed into
our jubilee outfits. I was excited
about my new red-and-gold
dress. Frosting was not as happy
about his outfit. He looked good
in his new red jacket, but I could

tell he was uncomfortable.

"Are you ready now, Cupcake?" Frosting asked.

Cupcake checked herself in the mirror one more time. She started to brush her hair ... again. "Almost," she said.

Frosting shook his head from side to side. "We have to get to the stables," he said. "Your hair looks fine."

"My hair has to look better than fine today," she snapped.

"Let's go see how Sparkle is doing," I said. I knew Cupcake would want to check on Sparkle.

Soon we were all out the door.

There was already a large crowd of Candy Fairies in the castle courtyard. Castle Guard Fairies were standing in rows with long golden sugar trumpets and color-ful flags for each of the kingdoms. I spotted my parents, **Princess Lolli** and **Prince Scoop**, and my aunt Sprinkle next to my grand-parents. They were seated on the stage at the far end of the square.

I waved. My wings were flutter-ing extra fast. I had never seen so many Candy Fairies in one place. I turned to the side gate and saw Gobo and Taffy walking into the courtyard.

Sparkle was next to Jelly. All

the royal unicorns were lined up.

Frosting and I took Sparkle to the front of the castle. Cupcake went to get the banner ready. Gobo and Taffy were waiting in the courtyard.

"Here we go," I said to Sparkle.

Frosting and I walked her up the ramp to the castle. I could hear the trumpets inside.

I gave Sparkle a tight squeeze. "You can do this," I told her.

Frosting walked her up the drawbridge so she could make a

special entrance into the courtyard. Sparkle flew off. Her horn
lit up in rainbow colors, and the
crowd of Candy Fairies cheered.

"She did it!" Frosting exclaimed.

Sparkle took a lap around the courtyard. She looked so joyful as she flew. She was making many Candy Fairies happy, especially my grandparents.

Later, Flour and Jelly flew through the obstacle course. I

was amazed to see how Flour flew Jelly in and out of the rainbow hoops and jumps. With each trick, the crowd cheered louder and louder. At the end, Cupcake, Frosting, Taffy, Gobo, and I held up our banner.

"We love you! Happy Rainbow Jubilee!" we shouted.

Sparkle flew over to Frosting and Cupcake. She nuzzled their shoulders. I couldn't believe this was the same unicorn who wouldn't fly a few days ago!

"We knew she was different," I said. "We didn't know how different!"

"That was **sugar-tacular**!" Taffy cheered.

"Sparkle was the star!" Gobo exclaimed.

Flour flew over to us. She petted Sparkle's head. "How did you get her to fly?" she asked.

"A little bit of luck and a little bit of hard work!" I told her.

"A real rainbow surprise," said Cupcake.

Flour rubbed Sparkle's nose. "You did a super job training her," she said. "Being a rainbow unicorn makes her even more special."

Cupcake and Frosting were smiling. We flew over to the stage when the show was over.

"I haven't seen a rainbow unicorn in many years," Grandma Sweetie said.

"How did you keep this a secret?" Grandpa Crunch asked. "You all are supersweet!"

Princess Sprinkle agreed. "This makes today even more **rainbow-licious**," she said.

My cousins, Taffy, Gobo, and I were very proud of the work we'd done to help Sparkle fly.

But we were most proud of Sparkle herself.

Being with friends and family helps make a celebration even sweeter!

Happy anniversary to Queen Sweetie and King Crunch!

Word List

comfortable (CUMF•ter•bull):
Relaxed

drawbridge (DRAW•brij): A
bridge that can be raised, let
down, or drawn to the side

drooping (DRU•ping): Hanging
or sinking down

grazing (GRAY•zing): Feeding
on grass or other leaflike plants

grunted (GRUN•ted): Made a
deep, short sound from the throat

harness (HAR•ness): A set of

straps for a unicorn or horse

heap (HEEP): A large pile

mane (MAIN): The long hair on the neck and head of a unicorn, horse, or other animal

moat (MOTE): A deep, wide ditch surrounding a castle that is usually filled with water

nuzzled (NUH•zuld): Touched or rubbed one's nose against

paddock (PA•dock): A field where animals like horses are kept

showcase (SHO•kays): To display in a pleasing manner

smirked (SMURKD): Smiled in an unpleasant way

solution (suh•LOO•shun): An answer to a problem

turrets (TUR•itz): Small towers of a castle

unique (you•NEEK): Unlike anything else

wobbled (WAH•buld): Moved in an unsteady way from side to side

Questions

1. What kind of celebration is happening in Sugar Kingdom?
2. How would you train a unicorn?
3. What treat did Gobo give Sparkle?
4. What gift would you give Queen Sweetie and King Crunch?